# Kaylee's Secret Mission

Sue Carpenter

Sue Carpenter

# Contents

# Chapter One
## A New life

November 2011

I stopped inside the doorway of my new bedroom. This was my room? It looked twice as big as the tiny caravan I'd shared with Mum. The thick carpet sank softly beneath my feet as I crossed to the enormous four-poster bed and sat down. I clutched at one of the white posts at the corner of the bed and leaned my forehead against it. None of this seemed real. I ran my hand over the pale pink and white striped bedding. It felt real; smooth and creamy and plush. Across the room, a couch with matching fabric stood in front of a wide window, framed by curtains in the same luxurious pattern. It was as though I'd been transported into a home and garden catalogue. I picked up a cushion from the plush mountain resting at the bed's headboard and hugged it to my chest. It was surprisingly soothing, but right now I'd give anything to be sitting next to Mum on our shabby old couch, resting against one of the patchwork cushions she'd sewn from scraps of old material. Not one of those cushions matched another, but they had been infused with love and packed with memories. I needed to get ready for life with my newly found father and my older brother, Paul. Easier said than done.

Earlier today, I'd arrived in Auckland for the first time, glad to have survived the plane trip. As far as I was concerned, getting from A to B above the ground was wrong. My new house was so enormous, I wondered how I would manage to find my way down for breakfast in the morning, or would I accidentally stroll into a broom cupboard by mistake? I was the first child born this millennium, and Mum always said that's why I was bad with directions. And clumsy. And anything else, it was my standard excuse and one that never made sense.

I couldn't stop thinking about Mum. It had been only one month since the two of us had walked along the beach, arm in arm, and she told me we didn't have long left together. It had been just one week since I'd said my farewells and buried her.

Cancer was so cruel. Not sharing this new experience with her was so wrong. It was also wrong for her not to kiss me good night, and wrong for her not to laugh at me when the inevitable happened, like when I ended up in a broom cupboard the next morning.

Last week, Mum told me she was worried about my future and where I would live when she moved on. We had no other family, but we had the people that lived by us, and to me, they were my family. She'd flown to Auckland alone, easily found my father he had a fifteen-year-old daughter. Mum also told him she was dying and didn't have much time left. My father had instantly pulled Paul out of work, and the three of them had caught the next plane to Invercargill to meet me.

From the minute Mum arrived back, she was bedridden. That trip had cost her every last ounce of energy.

As Mum hadn't told me anything about my father, it had never even occurred to me to ask. So, meeting him (and Paul) had shaken my world, I'd always thought I would live with someone else in the camping ground when Mum moved on, not this huge move to live with blood-related strangers.

Mum and I saw the world through the same glasses, and we were so similar in personality and attitude, but never in looks. Mum was shorter than me and so petite. And that was saying something. She had thick, wild, unmanageable red hair and freckles with topaz eyes. My auburn hair was fine, and I had green eyes. The same look I now knew my father and brother had.

So, there I was, still sitting in the enormous room within this unfamiliar massive house. Just me, my one little suitcase, my small box of treasures. Somehow, I was meant to fill this room up and make it feel like it was mine with my few belongings. I laughed to myself (and Mum would be laughing too) as I hung the dress Dad had bought me to wear to Mum's funeral. (I had no intention of ever wearing that again!)

I also hung three old tee shirts, a pair of jeans, shorts, and my hoodie on the rail and

I put my one pair of shoes on the shoe rack in the huge walk-in wardrobe.

I'd wanted to bring some of Mum's clothes with me, but sadly, I'd outgrown them. It would have been wonderful to have worn her pyjamas to bed, or on a freezing day snuggle in one of her hoodies or cardigans. I was too broad-shouldered.

Joshua had helped me try. There wasn't a single item of Mum's clothing that I could fit, only her locket.

My gigantic new wardrobe appeared even bigger once I hung my handful of clothes in it.

It didn't take long to put my pyjamas and underwear away in the top three drawers leaving the other six empty.

'This is crazy,' I said to myself, 'now to the box.'

I placed the photo of Mum and me at the beach on my drawers, took out my diary, and Susie Spy books, and put them on the desk with my special painting.

The only thing left to do was to lie on the bed and stare at the painting until it was too hard to see through my tears.

Mum and I had never had a lot of money for photos, so when we found out she was going to, well, shall I say move on to another existence, together we painted a memory canvas.

It had all our memories painted on it, our holidays, my childhood things like my first word had been crocodile, so we drew a crocodile.

Mum had been a renowned artist, and she did an amazing drawing of our old cat who had died a year before she did.

I stared at the painting and remembered every story the brush strokes told.

I moved the painting to my big white and very bare desk and threw myself back on the bed. That was when I lost it (well, for the first time since the funeral anyway).

Why, why, why! How could life be so cruel? How could I survive without the one lady who truly understood me? The people who held me weren't my mum. I needed my mum, not a change of address. My best mate, Joshua, would have been more helpful than these foreign family members. No one could help; not really! No one could bring my mum back to me.

After I lay there crying for ten minutes, there was a knock at the door.

'Come in,' I sniffled.

Paul entered my room.

'Oh, hi Paul,' I sobbed, still choked up.

He swept me up and gave me a big hug, 'Oh my sweet honey, wipe those tears away, how about you and I go to the mall, get you some more things to personalise your room, turn it into more a Kaylee styled room instead of an empty room? And we can get you some new clothes because we have a fancy dinner on Friday night, and you will need something glamorous to wear. Does that sound like a plan?'

I had a chuckle to myself. Surely Paul must have seen the bare wardrobe and shopping jumped into his mind. I know Joshua would never offer to take his sister shopping. From what I'd experienced with boys, shopping just wasn't their thing.

Surprisingly, it was better with Paul there. 'Sure, I guess,' I replied casually. It had to be better than sitting there feeling sorry for myself, that was for sure.

# Chapter Two
## So Many Shops

We slid into Paul's brand-new black Audi and drove to the mall.

'Do you like your new room?' he asked me.

I think he found the silence uncomfortable; I was enjoying looking around at the houses, people, even the dogs I found interesting. Oh, why would anyone have a dog that could fit in a handbag? A concept that was beyond me. I laughed aloud when I saw a dog wearing a raincoat. Poor thing!

Paul looked and chuckled, too.

'Do you like your room?'

'Yes, thanks,' I replied. 'I'd never dreamt bedrooms could be that big and have their own bathroom, too. It's bigger than our entire trailer back home.'

I slipped back into silence, thinking about everything that I'd left back home, especially all my amazing friends and neighbours. My new house had such tall fences that I could hardly even see the neighbours.

'You know how I said we have a big dinner tomorrow night, well I have an enormous secret, but I would like to share it with you.'

'What is it?' I asked, intrigued.

'Well, you know my girlfriend, Barbara? Last night, we talked about getting married.'

'Oh Paul, how great. Congratulations!'

'Cheers, the dinner is to announce the engagement and to plan the wedding.'

'She seems nice, and jeez, is she ever pretty?' I'd only met her once, but she had been friendly, nearly too friendly, which was weird.

Barbara was thin, bronzed skin and had big blonde hair and by big, I mean big! Just like Fran from the nanny, but blonde, not black. (The nanny had been Mum's favourite TV programme.)

'Barbara decorated your room,' Paul continued, 'but I think it looks a bit like it belongs in a magazine. That's why I planned to sneak you out to buy some other things for it.'

'Thanks,' I said before slipping back into silence. Auckland was big, but the mall wasn't too far away from their home.

'Do you like to read, Kaylee? Your bookshelf looks lonely, with only four books on it. Shall we start there?' He pointed to the bookstore as we pulled in at the mall.

'Oh yes please, I would love to get another Susie Spy book to read if that's ok? Our second-hand bookshop hasn't had any new ones in ages.'

'Reading is very important in our house. It's important to us that you have books to read. We often have reading time as family time.'

Some kids at my old school would have hated that – not me.

The mall was gigantic, 'Oh my gosh, I have never seen anything like this, so many shops altogether.'

The mall, as they called it, was larger than the whole township back home, and the bookshop was huge, with two levels of books and stationery. 'I could easily spend all day in here,' I laughed as I saw that was what people were doing. There were couches placed around the shop and even a cafe. I'd have to write to Maddison back home and tell her all about the shop. She loved reading as much as I did.

Paul walked to the counter and spoke to the saleslady. 'My sister here would like one of each of the Susie Spy books you have in store.'

'All!' I gasped.

The sales lady got a box set out from behind her and then got another book and said, 'This is the latest. It has only been out a few days.'

Paul turned to me and said, 'So, what else do you read or have interests in?'

'I used to read whatever I could get in the second-hand shop back home, whatever was available, and I loved everything I read. I love mysteries, drama, fantasy, art and dancing,' I replied.

I felt like I was in a dream and I'd won a shopping spree.

Paul asked the lady, 'Can you please get together a collection of books, and a few books on living in Auckland? My little sister just moved here yesterday. I will be back to pay in a few minutes.' The sales lady was frazzled, and I would have hated to have seen how shocked I looked.

We left the bookshop and headed into the next shop, 'Teen Queen.'

In there, there were more clothes than I'd ever seen, and all-new, not second hand as I always had had before. Paul asked the saleslady to help me find a completely new wardrobe.

Again, my eyes almost jumped out of my head.

While feeling like a princess, I tried on everything. Eventually, we left the store with two pairs of new jeans and a pair of smart black trousers, two pairs of shorts, six tee-shirts, some smarter than others, two pairs of pyjamas (one pair was silk), two pairs of togs, (Paul had said I would use their pool loads), a summer dress and a nice formal dress for the dinner tomorrow night.

In the meantime, Paul had gone back to pay for the books and put them in his car. He arrived back with a trolley and a silly grin. 'Your challenge is to fill this up,' he said, 'but first, how about ice cream? Here they make these in front of you and you can have any flavour you like.'

'Oh yes, please.'

There were so many flavours to choose from but in the end, I tried boysenberry.

Paul and I talked about spy gear. He had said one of his friends and his brother used to leave clues and notes around the house for each other when they were younger, and they had loads of fun. That sounded cool. As we talked, Paul had slipped into a second childhood. We laughed loads... it was therapeutic.

While we were enjoying the most amazing ice cream I'd ever had and chatting away, I thought I saw Paul's fiancée, Barbara, at a cash machine. But instead of the designer clothes and buffed hair that she normally wore, this lady had long straight flat red hair and was wearing hippieish clothing. Just as I decided that there was no way it could have been Barbara, from the corner of my eye I saw the lady see us. Her face went pale.

I imagined beads of sweat forming. The lady looked over at a group of people and then twirled her back. She left the mall in a huge hurry.

So bizarre.

I was still thinking about the strange actions of the lady when Paul interrupted my train of thought by saying, 'Let's go into this toy shop and get walkie talkies. Then we can chat to each other in our own rooms at night.'

Paul had not noticed the Barbara lookalike, and I soon forgot all about her once I saw the huge toy store.

Together we happily walked into the toy shop and bought invisible writing pads and pencils, walkie talkies and a selection of other such spy toys.

Paul could not resist. He also bought me a full-size teddy bear which had caught my eye. It was the most beautiful bear. I was so amazed by it, and as if that were not enough, he bought me a lot of other toys.

With a giggle I said, 'Now my spacious room will not feel so big. Thanks so much, Paul.'

Next was a jewellery shop.

'Kaylee, Dad wanted me to buy you a charm bracelet,' Paul explained.

'What is that?' I replied.

'It is a bracelet you buy charms for. Look, see, here are some charms—a magnifying glass, ballet shoes. Get them. How about a teddy bear to represent me like this big one?' he pointed to the bear he had bought me which filled most of the trolley.

'Oh yes, and may I please have the paintbrush charm, because Mum loved to paint,'

'Absolutely.'

Together we chose a kiwi, silver fern, the Sky Tower, and a beautiful bracelet to put them on.

'Paul, Mum had a locket. Can I put that on my charm bracelet, too?' I asked.

'Oh, it's perfect. Is it gold or silver?'

'Gold,' I replied, and I opened my wallet and lifted it out.

The salesperson commented on my amethyst, and he offered to put that on as well.

I was so happy. Mum had given me this crystal the morning she moved on. She said it would help me go forward into my new life.

I handed them to the man. He said it would take thirty minutes for him to put all the charms on the bracelet and asked if we could wait.

'Oh, I can't let you buy me anything else, Paul! You have bought me so much. More than I have ever dreamt of. Thank you so much, but I think we should go soon. I have no money to repay you.'

Paul smiled and gave me a big cuddle and laughed, 'Honey, you are an Edwards now. Dad is paying for all of this, and you don't need to worry about money again, okay, sweetie? Now, let's buy this lot and then go get you some paints, canvases, and anything else you need for your desk.'

I hugged Paul back. Together we spent the rest of the day shopping and laughing and getting to know each other.

Paul had to empty the trolley twice more.

On the way home, I asked Paul if we could stop off at the beach. I love my new bracelet, but the jeweller had touched my amethyst.

Crystals had healing powers. Mum had always believed in all sorts of spiritual things that Paul and Dad had never heard of, but crystals were important to Mum.

Mum had been a massage therapist. She would always use natural and organic products like honey, lavender, and any other methods. It always worked for her. I wish those methods could have saved her in the end.

Mum told me she would not have lasted as long as she did if she hadn't followed her alternative natural cancer treatment.

As we had been walking across the beach, I'd been so busy thinking about Mum that I'd forgotten Paul was even with me. Breaking my thoughts, he came and put his arm around me. 'Kaylee, I have to tell you, I love having you as a sister. I know our relationship is new, but I have always wanted a sibling and I think you are fantastic!'

I smiled and fought back the little tear which was forming in my eye. I leaned to the saltwater, and as I did, I explained to Paul how the saltwater purifies the crystals of any negative energy and vibrations.

Back at home, it took Paul and me three loads up and down the stairs to put all the bags in my room.

Paul had some work to deal with, so I was left in my room unpacking all the goods alone.

The drawers were filled.

My bathroom now had nice rose-soaps, body washes, and hair accessories in the drawers as well.

Even my shoe rack was much fuller, with two new pairs of shoes, some boots, sandals, and slippers.

I put my art supplies away and the gigantic bear on my bed. At least the bed would not feel so big.

It would be funny to call the bear after Paul, so I got the fabric paint we had bought, and I wrote Pauline on the bear's left paw.

I stood back and checked out my room. Not only did it have more personality in it, it felt more like me. Turning to look out the window, I saw the swimming pool. Paul was right. I would love to spend time there, but swimming was more fun with friends. My friends were miles away. A movement caught my eye, from the neighbour's house. I could see straight into a boys' bedroom. He was at the window too and waved to me.

I waved back. Then turned from him and kept looking around the neighbourhood. When my eyes moved back, the boy was holding a gigantic piece of paper that said *hello*.

I smiled.

I sat at my desk and on a piece of paper I wrote *hello* too, and I drew many flowers and trees on the paper. He was still there with another piece of paper as I headed back to the window. *I am Mason,*

I showed him my *hello*.

Sitting again, I wrote my name on the paper.

Just as I'd finished, Paul came to see how I was going.

He laughed at the teddy bear's name, too.

Paul and I had the same sense of humour, which was cool. I knew he would get along well with my best mate, Joshua. Oh, how I missed Joshua.

Paul helped me hang my special painting, which I'd told him all about.

Then the dream catcher Mum and I had made when I was five years old, and we put some photos in frames on the bookshelf, including the picture of me and Paul we had taken in the mall at a photo booth.

Paul put one in a frame too for himself and said, 'See you at dinner. I am off to put this in my room,' as he waved our photo at me.

Back at the window, Mason wasn't there, so I taped my name to the window before spending some time trying on my new clothes and shoes in different combinations and putting them back in their new homes. Finally, I chose a casual pink tee shirt and blue jeans, my new charm bracelet, and a necklace to wear for dinner.

Dad had an important job. I did not understand it, but he was a powerful man and would have to go on many trips to Wellington to the Beehive, as well as overseas, where he represented New Zealand somehow.

He worked long hours, and I'd looked forward to him coming home that night.

Dad, Paul, and I sat around the table and had a three-course meal as we talked about our day shopping and what we had purchased. We didn't tell Dad about the walkie talkies, invisible pens, and other spy gear, as that was Paul's and my secret.

After dinner, we all had a swim and then I took Dad and showed him my new room and what we had bought.

He told me he had to go to Christchurch early tomorrow for the night, but would be back before the big dinner on Friday night.

Paul had my day planned for tomorrow, but I would have to wait to find out what it was.

Dad kissed me good night, and I slept better than I had since the passing of my mum.

# Chapter Three
## Clues

The following morning, I woke to a letter.

*Good morning,*

*Today I have several things to do with you. The first is... you have to solve your clues by the time Barbara gets here at 10 am. So, you have from now till then to work out where we are going, and to dress accordingly.*

*There is a clue in every room on the bottom floor of the house.*

*An invisible map included.*

*Good luck*

*Love Paul*

*P.S. Bring your new camera with you.*

New camera? I focused on my desk and there was a present.

I jumped out of bed and opened it. There was a hot pink digital camera with a hot pink laptop to match.

At school, we had learnt all about computers, but I had never had one in the caravan. Unboxing the camera, I plugged it in, turned it on and took a photo. Then I remembered I needed to find out where we were going.

There was a note on Mason's window. *Where are you from?*

I wrote back *Invercargill, but live here now.*

Oh Boy, I had to have breakfast. I always lose track of the time and still need to get dressed, too.

Just as I was about to have a shower (in my room, how weird) there was a knock at my door. Our housekeeper, Pepe, was there with my breakfast, so I ate in bed. Breakfast in bed! After my strawberry smelling shower, the treasure hunt began.

I headed downstairs.

According to the map, there was a rumpus room, entrance, study, guests' room, and library. This would be the first time I'd been in any of these rooms except the entranceway.

I decided to work anti-clockwise, as the library was the room I most wanted to see.

Weird, I'd lived there for two days and did not even know we had a library. It sounded strange saying I lived there. It would take a lot of getting used to. This place was as far from Mum's little caravan as I could get.

So, to the first room. This room had two walls of books. Everywhere there were books. I'd never seen so many books in my life, (well except for that amazing bookshop yesterday) and there were loads of chairs and even bean bags. Some chairs were big recliners, some leather armchairs, some had amazing cushions on them too.

The cushions were either cross-stitched or patchwork, and they all looked homemade, which made the room feel cosier.

There must have been a chair, couch, or beanbag to suit every type of person, and there were a few side tables next to some chairs. I had a look at these. One book was open on elephants, another was also open on elephants. As I hunted around, all the books on all the tables had elephants on them, and there were even some elephant books on the beanbags.

Wow! One clue must be elephants. I began to get excited. I loved elephants but had never seen one. Maybe we were going to the zoo.

'Slow down, chick,' I said to myself. I'd better not get too excited, as it may be an elephant movie.

A movie would still be great.

The next room had an adjoining door, and it was Dad's study. A very empty room.

I was out-of-place being there, like I was being nosy, and was about to get a beating for even thinking about being in here. Not that Dad looked like that kind of man, but it was early days.

I didn't know any of these people, or should I say, family.

Back to it, there was a leather chair sitting in front of the fireplace (the fireplace was double-sided with the library) and an enormous desk with one leather chair on one side and two visitor's seats on the other side.

There were three framed photos. One of the late Mrs Edwards, one of Paul, and much to my surprise, one of me taken a few Christmases ago.

Mum must have given it to Dad.

Sitting on the desk was a zoo brochure.

Yes! We must be going to the zoo. Woo hoo!

There was an animal park close to Invercargill; it had a tuatara and kiwi and a few other native animals which I loved, but no monkeys, tigers and certainly no elephants.

I walked back into the entrance and passed the piano and the grandfather clock. I had a quick look around, but nothing, like a clue, jumped out at me. Then I headed into the opposite doorway. It was the rumpus room.

Oh, my gosh!

What a massive room. It had a bar, a billiard table, and a darts board.

All the glass doors opened to the outside, where there was the swimming pool.

It surprised me when familiar opera music playing quietly reached my ears. I was the only one around. I walked to the stereo and saw a CD *Phantom of the Opera*. and then I remembered the piano in the entrance room had sheet music on it, so I rushed back out to the piano.

Sure enough, it was Phantom of the Opera sheet music.

I'd seen the movie on TV once in black and white. It was magical, but never in my wildest dreams had I thought I would ever see anything like that live. 'Better not get my hopes up,' I said to myself.

I danced to the music; I'd not danced for months and was getting lost in the notes.

I sang as I danced around the room, till the doorbell rang. It jolted me back to reality.

Oh, dear, if that was Barbara, I was so not ready! I ran into the next room, which thankfully was the last room downstairs.

This was the spare bedroom for visitors. In there, sitting on the dressing table, were three third-row tickets for the Phantom of the Opera at six o'clock that night.

Wow! I ran upstairs and into my room, where I got ready.

Laid out on my bed was the most beautiful dress I'd ever seen, with a note from Paul saying, *Hope it fits you. See you soon.*

I glanced at the time. It was 9.57.

I threw on the same jeans and tee I'd worn to dinner last night. (There was no point wearing new ones as they were not dirty yet.) I grabbed my new bag, complete with the camera, and ran back into the entrance with less than two minutes to spare. Not that it mattered. Paul and Barbara were already there chatting when I ran to them both and gave them big hugs.

'I don't know if I have ever had this many hugs,' Paul laughed.

Barbara hugged me back, but the hug felt awkward. Note to self, ease off on the Barbara cuddles. Some people just feel violated about having others in their personal space, but I'd never been.

Back home in Invercargill, I walked around hugging and holding hands all the time, with everyone.

'Are we going to the Zoo and the Phantom of the Opera?' I asked.

'We sure are,' Paul replied, 'but did you miss a clue?'

'The elephants at the Zoo, and the Phantom?'

'Yes, you got them all, but misinterpreted one. You are not only going to see the elephants, I booked us on an elephant experience. You and I will get to touch and feed the beautiful beasts.'

My tummy did a happy dance. I'm going to see an elephant and touch it?

We drove to the Zoo, and I was silent in the car.

I wondered what the elephants would feel and smell like, how big they would be and how excited my mum would have been for me if she were still alive.

I would have to get postcards to send home to my friends, they would be blown away.

# Chapter Four
## Elephants

We got to the Zoo an hour before the Elephant experience, so we walked around and looked at all the animals. Paul shared a story with me about how his school ball had had cheetahs greeting everyone as they arrived in the hall. Sounded to me like the flash private school he'd been to was so different from my old school.

Barbara told me all about the dress she had worn that night, and the genuine diamonds sewn into it.

Barbara talked a lot about who would be seated next to who at the dinner the following night, and between what course they should share their news?

Paul kept interrupting her to tell me little interesting things about the animals, like tuataras can live to be over one hundred, and tiger's stripes are not just in their fur but on their skin too.

It was so lovely walking around the zoo. I was amazed at how tall the giraffes were.

It was feeding time for the zebra and ostriches (they were all in the same area).

We lined up and got to feed the giraffe. Its tongue was black and long, really long. I was shocked.

We continued around past the lions and elephants (which we would come back to), and the pink flamingos.

'Did you know pink flamingos are not pink when they are born but they eat so many shrimps that they turn pink, the same as if we eat loads of carrots? Our skin can turn orange.' Paul shared yet another interesting fact with me. He always smiled when he spoke with facts.

As we walked through the Ozzy walkabout, Paul was chatting again. In fact, I think I hardly said five words between Paul chatting about the animals and Barbara trying to side-track him with engagement plans.

Paul said, 'Now Kaylee, they say emus and kangaroos cannot walk backwards, but how can they know this?'

Barbara looked at her watch and said, 'What time is your elephant thing?' Paul looked down, too. 'Crap, Kaylee, we gotta run.'

We turned around and ran back through the walkabout, scaring the peacock, and back past the café.

'Paul, I will catch up with you there. You run ahead,' Barbara said as she turned into the bathroom. Paul grabbed my hand, and we ran. We still got there early. It didn't take long to run from one side of the zoo to the other.

The time goes quickly when you are not stopping to look at all the amazing animals.

We were recovering from our run when a lady in red arrived. 'Hi, you must be the Edwards?' she smiled. 'The keeper will be here shortly. Until then, pop in here and find some gumboots that fit you.'

The keeper arrived seconds later and ran us through the health and safety issues, and then we got to meet Burma, the elephant. To start with, we had to be still and quiet while she got used to our smell, then we gave her bananas and got to have photos with her.

Next, Burma got down on one side and we got to wash and scrub her clean (after a demonstration, naturally) and once we had finished that side, she got up, rolled over and we washed down the other side.

Next, we all walked outside to her outdoor area where the keeper did a public encounter and we watched from inside the field. It was all so impressive.

Barbara arrived; she took out a video camera and took some photos and a video for us. (But she spent a lot of time talking on her cell phone.)

This had to be the coolest thing I'd ever experienced, and I even learnt some interesting facts from someone other than Paul. Asian male elephants are called bulls, and the females are cows. Newborn babies weigh around 125 kg, about the same as three ten-year-old children, and elephants are the only animals that can't jump.

After the encounter, Paul bought an adoption pack (which included even more elephant facts, certificate, stickers, and a soft toy elephant) for me (so cool) and gave me an elephant charm to put on my bracelet. It was the most magical time.

On the way home, we took the photos to be developed. I could send my personalised postcard home to Joshua with a photo of me, Paul, and Burma. It didn't take long, so we tracked to the jewellers, and they added my elephant to my charm bracelet. While we waited for the photos and charm bracelet, we chilled out in the café.

Paul and I got a lot of talking done while Barbara was on her phone.

'Anyone would think her phone was glued to her ear,' Paul joked.

After getting home, I took the short walk to the beach to wash my bracelet. I loved being around Dad and Paul, but it was nice to be alone sometimes, too.

I was never alone back home and when I wasn't with Mum, I was with Joshua or one of the other neighbourhood kids. In fact, anyone from the park.

I also loved visiting the local oldies and hearing all their stories. Joshua loved hearing the war stories from old granddad Roger, while I loved learning how to cook from Aunty Julie.

Every resident was called uncle, aunty, or cousin; it was a really extensive family, which was what I needed around me when Mum was dying.

At first, when Mum told me about Dad and Paul, I was beside myself, happy to have a dad and a brother. But having to move was not what I wanted. I even hid from them for an hour, and Joshua and I spied on them. We decided they seemed like decent people, so we came out of hiding, but Joshua did not leave my side that first day they stayed in Invercargill.

As I arrived back at home (well, Dad and Paul's home) I walked around to the back entrance.

I paused. I could hear Paul and Barbara fighting, 'Look! Just stop and listen to me! Your sister, if that is what you are now calling her, is well, she's weird, and quite frankly I just don't like her!' Barbara snapped.

At first, I had to laugh because she was the weird one. Hadn't she just spent all day trying to get me to like her? And now she's acting like this. I wasn't sure what to think when Paul said, 'I understand you are used to having me all to yourself, but Kaylee is a part of my life now and always, and I want you two to be friends. She is not like you and me, but she is so special and her quirks like the crystals just make her more special.'

I was all choked up to hear him speak of me in such a loving way.

'Well, I think she is a little money hungry monkey. How do you even know if she is your sister, seeing your dad will not get the DNA tests?'

'Barbara, we have been over this before. All anyone has to do is look at her and me, to see we are related. If I put a wig on and a dress, we would be identical,' Paul replied.

I snuck around past them and headed to my room.

The first thing I did was look out the window.

Mason was there and waved as I took down my name.

He pointed to some paper which said *Welcome to Auckland.* He had drawn some pictures, too.

*Thanks.* I wrote and showed him.

He had already written back.

*How was your day?*

OMG. I wrote. How could I say I'd fed an elephant?

I picked up the toy elephant and pointed it at me, and played charades. I showed with the softtoy how we had got to wash and feed the elephant, and then I held up the photo. He got the general idea, even though he was too far away to see it.

He wrote back OMG!

Suddenly he turned in panic, and I moved back from the window. Another boy's face appeared. They almost looked like twins. Clearly, Mason was keeping our little chats a secret. I wonder why? I backed away more and had a shower. Not surprisingly, I smelled like an elephant.

My new dress fitted perfectly (seems weird saying 'new' as 99% of my belongings were new) I was ready to go to the phantom of the opera.

The dress Paul had chosen was orange, red and yellow and nothing I would ever have chosen or had ever seen before, but it looked great and suited me. Thankfully, I had some hair clips that matched, so I got dressed up.

I walked to the window, and Mason was waiting.

He put his hand on his heart and wrote *beautiful*.

His desk must be by the window as he could write replies without walking away like I had to. I held up the *thanks* from earlier and then wrote *opera*,

He gave me a thumbs up and wrote *enjoy*, before he waved again and was out of sight.

I sat at my desk and wrote a few signs in advance.

*How was your day?*

*have fun.*

*have a great day.*

I couldn't think of any others, so I made these signs and the thank you as pretty as I could and put them in a pile next to the window. Then I thought of one more... *good night.* And I drew it with stars and a moon on black paper using gold, silver and white pens. I even cut some stars out and taped it to the window.

Before I headed downstairs, I turned the desk lamp on and shone it on the sign, then I closed the door and found the kitchen for an early dinner. I was not sure how to react around Barbara now, but thankfully she was not there, and it was just Pepe and me.

'Come sit and have your dinner, honey.' She waved me over to the breakfast bar.

We'd only had dinner at the table in the other room so far, which was so formal; it was nice to eat there.

'I guessed you did not want to eat dinner in the big room by yourself,' Pepe said. 'And this way, we can chat while I do the dishes.'

'Sounds great,' I replied as I started to eat my macaroni cheese. 'Yum.'

'So, let us start with the most important thing, my dear. What do you love to eat and what do you dislike?' She filled the jug with water.

Well, what a hard question. 'I love pizza and chips, which was always the special meal we made for birthdays back home. We always ate whatever was in season. Most of the campers did seasonal work picking apples, cherries, or grapes. One meal I did love was a chicken and mushroom dish Mum would make with rice. But I have loved all your meals so far, Pepe.' I smiled.

'So, what, you eat anything? Brussels sprouts and all?' She teased.

'Yeah, any food should be treated as a privilege,' I said.

She laughed and said, 'My dear; you would be more suited to my house than here.'

'Where do you live, Pepe?' I asked.

'Before my husband passed away, we lived in Tauranga. It was great. I lived in a marae. My husband, Tane's family, was from there. It was a community not too dissimilar to yours from what I have heard. We ate as a community, and all helped each other out. I was a gardener and cleaner for the marae and Tane did the fishing. One day when he was fishing, a rogue wave hit him and, well, he never came home. The iwi was so supportive and helpful to me, but I did not feel comfortable staying there, so here I am, and I have lived here for fifteen years.'

I reached out and rubbed her arm. 'I am sorry to hear about Tane. So do you live here in this house? I think it looks too big just for two people.'

'No, you are just so sweet.' She walked me over to the window. 'See the cottage there? That's my place. Why don't you come to visit sometime?'

As I was about to say how great that would be, Paul and Barbara entered. Chatting to Pepe, I'd forgotten all about my earlier eavesdropping, as Mum would have called it, although Joshua and I always called it spying or sleuthing.

'You look amazing,' Barbara smiled an *over the top* smile, back to sucking up to me.

'Come on sweetie, we don't want to be late,' Paul said as he put his arm around me.

'Can I take you up on your offer tomorrow?' I asked Pepe.

'Naturally, see you at breakfast, honey. Have a wonderful time tonight,' Pepe replied.

Once in the car, Barbara asked, 'So, Kaylee, love, what wonderful thing has Pepe offered you?'

For the first time, I picked up on the sarcasm in her voice. As earlier, when Paul put his arm around me. She gave me a nasty look.

I could fake a smile, too. 'Pepe was telling me about herself, what an amazing person she is... well, she offered to show me her cottage.'

'Oh really, that's lovely,' Barbara replied. 'It's nice you are making new friends.'

Wow! What a weird thing to say. Friends? Pepe could be my grandmother.

One thing I am sure of was that Pepe didn't talk about me behind my back, or I hope she didn't. I would have said that about Barbara too... until yesterday.

Joshua always said I was too naïve for trusting people.

'But,' Barbara continued after a long pause, 'beware of her. Some money has gone missing around the house in the last six months, and it just must have been...'

Paul interrupted in a voice I'd not heard him use before, which scared me a bit. 'I asked you not to bring it up again. Kaylee, some things have gone missing lately, but there is no evidence of who it may have been, and we are not pointing our fingers at anyone.' He shot another stern look at Barbara and the rest of the car trip was in silence, but we were nearly there.

The opera building itself was the most amazing thing I'd ever seen. The theatre entrance had elephants and many other decorations on the walls. Paul, Barbara, and

I were there a bit early, so we sat in the cafe. I had my first ever Coke, as Paul and Barbara each had a glass of wine. Coke was, well, bizarre tasting, fizzy and unlike any other flavour I'd had before.

I would like to try it again sometime in the future. 'Yummy.'

Paul told me all about the wonderful history of the civic theatre, and then we glided in.

In the first half, I just sat there mesmerised. Watching every dance, every movement, and wondering how they could move around like they were. The stage had lights, smoke and stars, and everything looked like it was moving as it did on TV.

There were so many scenes, but everything flowed perfectly, and wow could the dancers dance, and singers sing. I jumped out of my seat when I thought the chandelier was going to fall on my head at the end of the first half.

At half time, Barbara left and got us all ice creams and I told Paul about the ballet I had been to last year. I had been performing while Mum was having chemotherapy and dancing helped me escape the reality of having an ill mum. Paul told me he would look into dance classes in the area and how it would be good for me to meet some friends up here. When the second half started, I was so captivated that I could not eat my ice cream. Paul finished it for me.

I fell asleep on the car ride home. It had been a full-on day.

Still half asleep, I heard Barbara say to Paul, 'I hope we are not babysitting the little brat again tomorrow. We have so much to plan, and she is just getting in the way.'

'Did nothing I say to you before sink in, honey? She is not a brat at all. Planning can wait. I am loving getting to know my little sister. I'll drop you off at your place tonight. I have some work to do.'

I smiled to myself as I heard this and fell back to sleep.

The next thing it was morning time. Wow, two good nights' sleep in a row, shocking.

# Chapter Five
## Friends

There was a charm on my bracelet after I woke with another invisible message beside my bed saying good morning. I laughed; I would've thought Paul was sick of taking me to the beach to wash my bracelet.

There was a knock at the door.

It was Paul. 'I have Dad online to say good morning,' and he showed me how to use Skype on my computer and the three of us had a big talk all about elephants and operas.

Dad said he had an old laptop lying around and he would send it to Joshua. I was so excited, I could keep in touch with him like this. I was so happy, and I thought of all the things I had to tell Joshua, from the elephants to shopping to the dancing, even though dancing was not his thing, but he would still love to hear all about it.

We said goodbye to Dad.

Paul and I had breakfast together. I asked about Barbara, and he said their relationship began when they started seeing each other in school. He had not even realised they were dating. They went to the ball together and, well; she has been with him ever since.

She kept asking when they would get married, so he guessed it was the next natural stage.

Tonight, they would announce their engagement and the wedding would be in three months, in February. Paul had wanted to backpack around the world, but Barbara told him he needed to stay close to Dad after losing his mother.

'How about you get dressed, and we walk next door and meet the neighbours?'

Which neighbours? Mason? Maybe other neighbours. What would I wear?

Paul continued, 'I have only ever waved at them, so it will be good for both of us to formally meet them. There is a secret message, but you can do it after lunch when

Barbara is fussing over the dinner plans, but please keep out of her way as you will be in the same areas as her.'

Running upstairs to my room, I headed straight for the window and took off the *good night* sign, and added *have a good day*.

Mason wasn't there, but there was a *how was the opera?* sign.

Twenty minutes later, Paul and I were walking next door to introduce ourselves. If we were both nervous, neither of us showed it. In this light, we both had a similar appearance (as Paul usually wore dress trousers, but today he had on jeans and a tee-shirt. same as me.)

A beautiful girl in her late teens with shoulder-length brown hair and stunning blue eyes answered the door.

Paul lost his words for a moment and then continued with, 'Hi, uh, I am Paul Edwards from next door, and this is my little sister Kaylee.'

'Hi, I'm Erin. We know who you are,' she paused, 'but did not know you had a sister.'

'Yeah, we didn't know 'til a few weeks ago, but it's great news. Anyway, Kaylee moved to Auckland two days ago and I think you have a sister about her age, so we thought we would come over and introduce ourselves,' Paul said.

'Sure thing, please come in.'

Once we were in their lounge, Erin called out, 'Amber.'

A girl my age came and said hi. She looked like a mini-Erin, but she had long hair.

The four of us sat and chatted. I explained how I came to live next door.

Amber and I hit it off straight away. Even though we'd both been raised worlds apart, we had many things in common. We had been chatting for half an hour when Erin said, 'We were about to have a game of Twister. Would you like to join in?'

'Yes please,' I replied. Joshua and I used to play it with his sisters. It was a genuine laugh.

Amber told me she had three siblings as Erin called out, 'Boys!'

We heard them before we saw them.

'What's your problem? The last few days you've been locked in your room all day. The only time you left is when you left to buy felts. What are you up to?'

'Nothing, just studying,' another voice replied.

'Sure you are!'

Then the two of them walked into the room.

My cheeks changed to apricot.

'These are my brothers, Jack and Mason,' Amber said.

Jack came to Paul, and me and shook our hands.

'I'm Paul. This is my sister Kaylee.'

'You live next door, don't you?' Jack said.

'Sure do,' Paul grinned.

Mason followed, shaking Paul's hand first and then mine. He winked and said, 'Hi, I'm Mason.' He squeezed my hand a little.

So, our messages are a secret, I liked the idea of that.

Her brothers almost looked like twins, well, except Mason, the younger one was taller. I swear Mason's eyes were the bluest eyes I'd ever seen.

Erin forced Paul into playing Twister, and everyone had a laugh playing, falling, and laughing.

After we had finished, they got their togs and came back to our place for a swim.

Paul and Erin talked about travelling. They both wanted to visit little places I'd not even heard about and backpack to places most people would avoid. The boys kept bombing and squirting everyone with water guns. They were such clowns, but in a good way.

Amber and I talked like we had known each other our whole lives.

While I was playing with Amber, I got distracted by a hissing noise followed by a voice saying, 'They had better not ruin our plan.'

I searched around, and it was none of us speaking in a high-pitched voice. I could see no one.

The boys made a large splash and covered Amber and me, so I lost my train of thought.

I already felt like Amber and I were the best of friends. But I also really enjoyed the company of both of the boys and Erin. So, in some ways, I had four new friends and could see their personality quirks. They wanted to chat with me too. Such a great family.

I didn't have time to talk to Mason alone, and he did not comment on our messages.

Too soon it became lunchtime, so the others headed back home, and Paul and I headed inside for lunch.

I ran to the room and saw *have a great day.*

*Fun morning.* I wrote, and I dotted Twister coloured dots on the paper with water splashes.

Smiling, I floated downstairs and sat next to Pepe. We ate together, and I told her all about the neighbours and the opera. Pepe told me I would have to wait till later to come to see her cottage, as Barbara had given her the day off. (I got the impression Pepe didn't like Barbara either)

Pepe was going to head out for the afternoon.

After checking to see if there was an additional note from Mason, which there wasn't, I started on my clues from Paul. The invisible map was of the second floor where Barbara was busy setting the table and arranging glasses and nibbles.

Excitedly, I set about my mission to complete my clues without being seen by Barbara.

Starting in the guest room, I found a gift addressed to me under the pillow. I placed it on the bed and continued to the next room. I saw Barbara coming, so I ducked into the walk-in pantry and, to my surprise, there on the bottom shelf was another gift wrapped in the same wrapping paper.

On my map, I put a cross on the pantry room and guest room and ducked back out, taking the two gifts upstairs to my room, before creeping down again.

Barbara was in the formal dining room, so I would have to be quick, as the lounge, kitchen and dining were all open-plan. There was a bookshelf with framed photos on it, but a new photo had been placed there. One of Paul and I, that was taken with the elephants, and on the back of the frame was a note from Paul saying, 'Thanks for one of the best days of my life yesterday, sis' and behind it, a little further back, was another gift.

This one fitted in my pocket, so I marked another cross on the area and walked towards the breakfast table. Footsteps got louder. I did a quick dive and roll behind the couch, a move that would have made any army instructor proud. It saved me from getting caught. Well, so I thought, until I snuck a peek to see where they were at. Paul winked at me. I smiled to myself.

And then they were gone again, but funnily enough, while I was sitting there, I found another gift under the couch. So, I ran those two upstairs, but on the way, made a stop in the guest bathroom and found a gift like the others. He did not hide it at all. It was a box as big as me, so I heaved those gifts upstairs and made another couple of marks with my pen. I still had the kitchen and formal dining room to go. Those would be the hardest if I wanted to stay out of sight from Barbara.

Everyone had moved to the kitchen, so I darted into the dining room. There was silverware everywhere on the table. How could somebody need that many knives and forks? I heard someone coming, so I hid behind the curtains.

While I was there, a phone rang. It was Barbara's voice that answered the phone. She said in a quiet and angry voice, 'I have told you not to call me. I will call you when it is safe... Yes, everything is going well and according to plan. It will soon be over and we will have everything that we have worked so hard for… Yes, you too. Call you later.' She hung up and left. My stomach dropped. What was she doing to Paul?

I glanced around for ages and couldn't find any gift, which was not too surprising, and Paul would not have wanted Barbara to see them in all her table decorating.

In the next room, I spied a gift on top of the tall cabinet. There was no way I could reach it up there, so into the kitchen I snuck. The only way to do the kitchen was to go there and sit at the counter and talk to Paul and scout around.

So, I did. And the gift was taped on the underside of the bar where I sat, so Barbara never suspected a thing.

I laughed aloud. Paul and I thought alike as the places the gifts had been hidden were places I would've put them.

Barbara snapped at me, 'What's so funny?' The way she spoke took me aback, but I replied, 'Yesterday, when we were in the car, I glanced out the window and saw three friends walking along. They all had the same outfits on, but in three different colours. They even had their hair done the same. It was funny.'

Paul laughed too.

Barbara just walked out of the room, and I heard her say, 'Honestly,' under her breath.

I asked if Paul could help explain the knives and forks to me in the dining room. Barbara said that was a great idea, but as she walked back in again, she gave us a three-minute time frame.

'Not fair, I can't reach that one,' I whined as we entered the room and I pointed at the gift.

'So, what do you think of the gifts?' Paul asked, and he reached up and passed me the present.

'Give me a break,' I laughed, explaining I'd not opened any of them yet and it was his engagement, so he should be the one getting the gifts.

Paul guided me to the elaborate table, quickly explained to me that I had to start with the cutlery on the outside and work my way in.

'Paul, time is up,' Barbara called, so I ran upstairs to open the presents. But I needed an engagement gift for Paul and Barbara, so I sat at my new desk to make one.

Using the art supplies Paul had bought me, I made a photo frame and headed outside to collect a lot of leaves and glue them around the frame. I added a lovely photo I had taken of them at the opera the night before.

Mason was at the window. *What are you doing?*

I laughed and held up the treasure map.

He drew back.

I didn't know how to explain but I drew an x on paper and using drama, I pretended to find the X.

I don't know if he understood, but he laughed, so that was close enough.

Now it was time to open the gifts. First, the biggest one was a telescope. I had always wanted one of these. Paul and I had talked about the stars last night before the Phantom started as the Civic Theatre had stars on the ceiling which were so magical. I couldn't wait till it got dark so I could watch them sparkle.

The second present was a pair of binoculars. I took them out and had a look-see out the window. I could see the neighbours Paul and I had met earlier that day out in their backyard, setting up for a barbeque.

'Oh, it must nearly be dinnertime,' I said to myself, so I got on the walkie talkie and asked Paul how long 'til I had to be dressed and be ready to go. His reply was, '20 minutes.'

There was enough time to open the last few gifts—a spy watch which had lots of cool things in it like a light, note area and mini voice recorder, there was a torch, and last, of all, there was a dancing outfit, shoes and a note saying he had booked me into the finest dance school in Auckland and I had lessons Tuesdays and Fridays after school.

# Chapter Six

## Dad talks about Mum

After I had a quick shower, I got dressed. There was a knock at the door. It was a frantic Barbara asking why I was not downstairs. People were asking to meet me, so I quickly placed my hair clips in my hair and pushed my feet into my shoes.

At the window, Mason held his heart again when he saw me all dressed up. But before I could communicate with him, Barbara rushed me downstairs. It was funny. A few steps before we reached the bottom, Barbara's tight and horrible grip on my hand turned into a loving soft grip, and her frustrated face was turned into a picture-perfect smile. I was sensing there was something not so nice about this lady at all. Barbara floated around, showing me off as a prize until my father arrived home. I was so happy I ran and hugged him.

He kept his arm around me while he, too, circled the room, welcoming everyone and explaining how the plane had been delayed and apologising for being late.

Then I got to have him alone for a few minutes. We went to his room. I sat on his chair while he got ready, and we talked about the neighbours and Wellington, before rushing back downstairs to the ballroom again, only to be escorted upstairs to the dining room by some waiting staff I'd never seen before.

Dinner was exceptionally long with lots of food I'd never dreamt about eating, but it tasted good (yet slimy). Snails, fish-eggs and duck. Before dessert, Barbara stood and said her big announcement, 'We are getting married.' Everyone toasted the happy couple. Over the pavlova and well into the night, Barbara told everyone about the wedding plans, and we were all surprised the engagement party would be held in a week and the wedding itself in two months. Some people said she may be pregnant, which I knew not to be true, as Paul had told me they were waiting until they got married for that kind of closeness.

The best part of the dinner for me was while everyone had coffee and cheese, my dad and I walked outside and had a big, long, deep, and meaningful chat.

'Kaylee, I want you to know I loved your mother very much,' he started. 'I was, of course, married to my wife at the time, but we were having a lot of marriage troubles. Paul was away at boarding school, and I was in Christchurch so often that my wife and I drifted apart, and as you know, your mum was the most amazing woman. We would run on the beach and do crazy things. When I was in Auckland, it was all boring suits and cocktails. With Tonia, it was carefree and impulsive and amazing.' Dad had a sweet smile on his face. It was clear he had loved both women.

'Tonia and I saw each other over a space of six months when I was in Christchurch, but then she said it would not work. She told me what to do to fix my marriage and sharply sent me back to my wife. For the first time in my marriage, it became fun because I never forgot her. I told my wife years later about your mum, and she was so grateful your mum had helped turn our marriage around. I have told most of this story to Paul, but I guess now he is getting married too, I should share some of the wisdom your mum gave me, so then he can have a great marriage like his mum and I had.'

People often told me than my mum had a way with words and used them to support others, but she talked her way out of giving me a dad. But at least she spread her wisdom far and wide while she could and had helped most who crossed her path, as she would say.

A while later, Paul found me sitting enjoying the view from the upstairs lounge, processing all of what Dad and Paul had told me, and going over my concerns with Barbara. Paul said the neighbours had called earlier and invited us to go on a tramp in the morning to the Waitakere ranges. This sounded fun, so Paul had said I would need to be ready at eight-thirty in the morning because I would need suitable footwear. We would have to go shopping again on the way. Then Dad asked if he could come. Paul said, 'Yeah, for sure. Their parents are coming,' Dad's face sparked. He had not been on a tramp for years and had not met the neighbours yet either.

Can you believe it took twenty-five minutes to say good night to everyone? In the window, next door, was a sign saying, *do you like tramping?*

I hung up my *good night* sign again and also a sign saying *yes*, then I headed to bed. But not before I focused the stars through my new telescope. As I did, I was incredibly surprised to see the flash of someone taking photos of the house. I grabbed my camera and snapped photos of him, but couldn't get close enough to see his face, or his car. I quickly got dressed all in black and tied my dark hair under a dark hat, and snuck downstairs. Outside and under the radar, I got some great close-up photos of the car, the man, and even his shoe print in the rose garden next to the kitchen window. On my new recording device I caught the mystery man saying, 'Should be enough photos to keep her happy,' before he got in his car and drove away. I darted back upstairs and loaded the photos and recordings under a new file on my pink computer, then put my PJs on.

# Chapter Seven
## Tramping

The alarm buzzed nice and early, but I'd already been awake for ages thinking about the mystery man and wondering if he had anything to do with Barbara.

*See you soon* was my sign this morning. I didn't have time to write back. I would see him soon enough.

When Paul came down, I was ready downstairs. He said Barbara was far too busy to join us, and she said for us to have an enjoyable time today. I felt bad that I was so relieved, she wasn't coming. So, Dad, Paul and I ate a big, healthy breakfast and packed some energy snack food and drinks, then we hit the road via the camping shop.

Paul was in a daze at the outdoors shop. He was smiling at the picture of the backpacks and admiring the technology of the tents and how little they could fold away.

Dad got me all kitted out with the best gear — all new clothes, socks, a pack— and he made me promise to go tramping at least one more time, so his money was not wasted. However, he also bought all the same gear for himself, so I joked with him he too had to go tramping soon and when he did... could I please go with him? We planned to go again after the engagement party next weekend. We all knew it was best to wait till after then.

We arrived at the tramping site at the same time as our neighbours were getting out of their van. Dad introduced himself, and we started the walk. Everyone naturally paired off. Jack and Mason charged ahead together, then Paul and Erin. Deep in chat, Amber and I, followed closely by the three parents. Everyone walked and chatted, stopped a few times to look at wetas and kauri trees. I was excited to hear Amber went to the same dance school I would go to, and we would be in the same class. 'It will be nice knowing someone on my first day,' I said.

'Don't worry, South, I'll look after you,' she joked. South had become my new nickname, as they thought it so funny I rolled my r's. I didn't even realise I did that.

We had a beautiful wood pigeon following us. He would swoop from side to side. And at one stage, he was joined by another one. At the bottom of the walk, there was a wonderful waterfall. Everyone dived in and swam. I took loads of photos and Paul commented to me about how he had never seen our dad this relaxed. It was like he had a new lease on life. We teased him, and he said it had been ages since he had been somewhere where he did not have to keep up appearances, or talk about the state of the nation, etc. The walk home was harder, all uphill, and everyone struggled. Well, no, not everyone. The boys and Erin didn't, but the rest of us did. However, we did all get back to the cars unharmed. Poor Paul had like thirty-five missed calls from Barbara. She had expected him home by ten and had not listened properly to where Paul had said we were going. Erin asked who Barbara was. Paul had just realised he had not once even thought about her, let alone mentioned her, so he told Erin he was engaged and a bit about Barbara as they got in their cars and carried on. The neighbours were heading off to Piha Beach for another swim, so we said we would catch up with them later.

'Mr. Edwards, can Kaylee please come swimming with us if she wants to?' Amber asked.

I nodded enthusiastically.

Dad turned to Amber's parents and said, 'Would that be alright?'

'We would love to take her,' they said, 'and there is more than enough room.'

Dad said 'thanks' to them and turned to me. 'Just make sure you swim between the flags and do not go out too far, you hear me?'

'Sure. Will do, thanks,' I added, smiling to myself. Dad cared about me.

I enjoyed going to Piha. I enjoyed doing family things and loved how the siblings teased each other.

On the way home, I felt a tickling feeling on my wrist. It was my watch. It had vibrated. Written on it where the digital time had been, it said: MESSAGE RECEIVED. I pressed a side button, *testing 123. Love Paul*, came on the screen. I pressed the same button. *How are you doing this?* I could type.

*I have the same watch. Cool eh?* he wrote, followed quickly by a *where are you?*

'Still at Piha. Are you at home?' I wrote.

'Yeah, Barbara has left me so many things to do, but she had to go to the cake shop.'

'Cool, we are in the van on our way home now. See you soon.'

The whole time I was writing to Paul, the boy's bright blue eyes were ogling the watch and chatting about it. Their parents had said they were only for adults and wouldn't let them have one. But they wanted to play with it. I handed the watch to them and continued talking with the girls while the boys messed with it.

'Kaylee,' Mason said, 'It even has games.'

Jack and Mason wanted them now, as they turned to tell their parents how neat they would be for Christmas, which was not too far away.

Amber said she wanted one, then she and I could chat too.

Just as I was about to send a message to Paul to ask him where he got them from, the van stopped at a roundabout in Titirangi. I was talking about the weird statues on the roundabout and took out the camera to take a photo. My eyes travelled to a couple kissing. 'They know they are in public, right?' I saw it was Barbara was kissing another man, in fact, the same one who had been taking photos the night before.

'That's Barbara!' Everyone followed my pointing finger. When Barbara saw the van of people looking her way, I ducked.

Barbara screamed in a horrible voice and not at all her normal fake sounding voice, 'What are you looking at, you bunch of loonies? Buzz off.'

I recorded it on my watch.

Over the next ten minutes, I told the others quietly so the adults would not hear us about the photographer last night, the intense phone call at the zoo, and in the dining room, as well as some of the other weird things that had been going on.

When they got home, Dad was sitting out on his deck reading the Weekend Herald, 'Kaylee, I don't like not being able to get hold of you. Not that I had anything to call you about yet, but maybe we should get you a phone. Do you want to get showered and dressed? Then I am going to take you out for dinner and buy you a cell phone. Does that sound good?'

'Yes, I would love to go out for dinner with you; I will go get ready as quickly as possible,' I said so excitedly. Everything seemed to get better and better except for the Barbara thing, that is. I have to admit, I felt much better having told the neighbours about it. They had said they would keep an eye out for any weird behaviour and let me know. They all had cell phones and had asked for my number; I could give it to them tonight, yay. Although I think I preferred chatting with Mason, the way we were now with the window messages.

The first thing I did back in my room was to turn the computer on, then I jumped in the shower and got dressed. I wrote a note *going out for dinner.* By the time I'd done all of that, the computer was revved up and ready to go. I saved the recording of grumpy Barbara and the photo of her kissing the photographer in the same file I'd placed last night's photos in, and then turned

the computer back off and ran downstairs
again.

On the way home from dinner, I was
playing with my new phone. I had already
worked out how to take a photo and record
things with it. It had much more memory
than my watch (just not as discreet). We
passed the yacht club where Dad told me
he usually goes on a Saturday evening. I
told him to drop me off at the gate and I
would walk in, and he could catch up with
his friends. 'I have a book I want to read
tonight if that's ok, Dad?' I asked.

As I strolled up the side of the driveway,
I could hear Barbara on the phone on the
upstairs balcony.

I could see Paul's car was not here, so
I snuck under the balcony and pressed
record. 'He had been talking about getting
married in a few years and going travelling
now, backpacking in Iran for crying aloud.
Who in their right mind would want to do
that? I always said he had to be around
to support his dad, but now that little brat
has arrived, he said we can travel. Over my
dead body, we are getting married as soon

as possible and then we can be on our way to being RICH AS. I'd better go. I've got a wedding to plan and life to ruin, ha, ha, ha.' Barbara hung up.

Sneaking upstairs, I added the recording to the others. As I lay on the bed, I tried to work out if I was reading into it more than I should be or Barbara was really up to no good. The last thing I wanted was anyone thinking I was attention-seeking, so if I spied more and collated it, then I could tell Paul when I had more information. I sorted out my spy gear and left some bugs around the house where Barbara often was. I was in the entranceway when Barbara saw me. 'Kaylee, what are you doing here?' she said, nearly yelling, then she caught herself and did the whole fake voice thing, 'Oh love, I thought you were out for tea with your dad.'

'Yes, he just dropped me off now. I thought I was home alone. I'm going to pop out to see Amber. See you soon,' I added as I popped out and headed next door.

The most worrying thing had been Barbara exiting Dad's study. What was she doing in there?

'Have you seen Paul? He's not answering his cell phone. I have been trying to get hold of him for ages. He should have been back an hour ago.' Barbara called behind me. It was in her charming voice now.

'No, but if I hear from my brother, I will let him know you are looking for him,' I said as I skipped off next door.

Barbara talked under her voice yet again. 'If you heard from him, he would have his phone and be calling me, you silly little freak.'

Bugger, I'd not got that on record, so I decided from now on I was going to be sickly nice to Barbara and drive her nuts.

I was super surprised to see Paul sitting in his car talking to Erin. Not sure why, but I took some photos of them. He was like a different man when he was with Erin — relaxed and happy. He laughed and appeared to have a sparkle in his eye. After ten minutes of watching them, I popped out of my hiding spot to say hi. I explained how Dad had gone out, then I had a thought. 'Amber was telling me about this amazing ice-cream shop in Mission Bay. Any chance you guys want to take me there?' They were both keen, and at the same time Amber had spied me from the house and came out to say hi. So Amber and I jumped in the back seat of Paul's car, leaving the front for Erin.

Once at the ice cream shop, I wrote a note under the table for Amber.

*We need an excuse to leave them alone; I will explain when we get away.*

Amber waited a few minutes, then said, 'Kaylee, have you seen the fountain?'

'Only by driving past it,' I replied.

'Can Kaylee and I go for a walk to the fountain with our ice creams, please?'

'Sure,' Erin and Paul said.

We cross the road to the beach side park. 'Okay, Kaylee, are you matchmaking? Paul is engaged.'

I explained to Amber all about the most recent conversations I overheard and how Paul had been flirting with Erin for ages and he was a different person when he was with her.

We had a great walk around the park and were gone for twenty minutes. When we finally got back, Paul and Erin had no idea how long we had been gone. They were still deep in conversation. Then my cell phone rang. It was Dad, which was not a shock, as he was the only person so far who had my number.

He said he had come home from the club after Barbara's fifth frantic call, saying she could not get hold of Paul. Oops, I'd completely forgotten to tell Paul how Barbara had been trying to find him.

Paul had left his phone in his jacket pocket in the boot of his car and could not hear it, so we all got in the car and headed home.

Before parting ways with the neighbours, I gave them my new number.

As you can imagine, I was thrilled when Paul said, 'Please don't mention the ice cream with Erin. Barbara would not understand.' I fully understood. He could not talk about Erin without a spring in his step. Did he have feelings for her?

Amber and I would have to make an official plan.... Bye-bye Barbara, Enter Erin.

# Chapter Eight
Pepe's story

The next morning at the breakfast table, Barbara called to say she could not go to church with them as she had a dress fitting, so I asked Paul if I could go with Barbara. Paul called Barbara back and, well, she couldn't say no.

Paul and Dad dropped me off at Barbara's apartment on their way to church.

You could imagine my shock to see the mystery camera operator was Barbara's flatmate.

Barbara said she would be five minutes getting ready and for me to make myself feel at home. So, I did Kaylee-style.

I had a nosy around when he went to the toilet, found some bills for Mrs Belinda Hooper which had *FINAL STATEMENT. If this bill is not paid, the debt will be passed onto a debt collector.*

There were a few like this and some for Mr. Scott Hooper, too.

I took lots of photos. There were a lot of photos of Barbara and her flatmate and none of Paul. There were two rooms, however, one was a spare room with dust on the bed.

'Let's go,' Barbara came out. She had not even noticed I'd been spying.

Her flatmate was angry. They probably had plans together. I'd seen them kissing yesterday.

We walked to the shop as it was just down the road.

Barbara did not have the appointment she had said she had, which I thought odd and suspicious, but the shop was happy to see her once she said who she was marrying.

Barbara tried a few dresses on — one made her look like a marshmallow, and I had a laugh with Barbara, but they were great on her. She was the picture of a Barbie getting married.

She shortlisted two and chose a veil and some other accessories and then had a look at some bridesmaids' dresses and got me to try a couple on. I had to hand it to Barbara when it came to fashion; she had great sense. She was very convincing with her friendly act. I almost forgot all about the *bye-bye Barbara, enter Erin* plan, as we were having a great time laughing together. This was the best side of Barbara. I wished she was always like that.

Barbara and I spent a morning giggling like old friends. Amber would be shocked.

That afternoon, Paul and Barbara talked about wedding plans. Barbara talked, and Paul was not paying a lot of attention to her and glancing in the direction of Erin's house.

Dad sat outside reading the Sunday papers, all three of them, and I had a refreshing swim, read my book, and had an internet chat with Joshua all about the goings-on.

At three o'clock, Pepe came and found me. 'I have some time before dinner if you still wanted that chat.'

'For sure,' I said as I followed her. First, she gave me a tour of the garden,

'This is my garden,' she said as she opened the gate.

'Wow.' It was an amazing, large, vegetable garden complete with compost and a worm farm. Beyond that garden was another gate.

Through the gate, there were loads of fruit trees. The plum trees were ready to be picked. 'I will make plum jam tomorrow if you have nothing on,' Pepe said as she handed me a small yellow fruit.

I watched her eat and then put the pips into another compost bin, so I copied.

'Yum,' I said, 'what is this?'

'Loquat's,' she said, 'The Edwards don't like them, so help yourself.'

'Can I please pick a bag for the neighbours?' I asked.

'For sure, I will give you some bags soon. Please feel free to pick them a bag of plums, too. We will not eat all of these.'

We had been eating a lot of fruit. 'Did you make the plum sauce we had for tea last night?' I asked.

'Sure did. Even the fruit you had with breakfast comes from here. When it's ready, I put it in a jar. I get real satisfaction from making it myself,' she went on to say, 'I even make your yoghurt. I would love chickens but have not managed to convince

Mr E yet.' Pepe's phone rang, so she left me wandering in the garden for a while.

This part of the garden made me feel like I was not too far away from home. This was definitely where I felt most at ease in Auckland. I would move a chair in here and make it my thinking spot, or private getaway. Some of the trees even had an area where I could crawl under and then stand up, like a play hut. Had Paul spent hours playing in here when he was younger? Probably not his thing.

Pepe came back out. 'Welcome to my home, Kaylee.'

I followed her in. It was amazing. A little two-bedroom cottage. All the chairs were covered in homemade quilts and wonderful paintings on the walls. One painting was of the vegetable garden and another of the trees I'd just been crawling under. 'Did you paint these? They are amazing.'

'I sure did,' she replied. 'I don't like having anyone else's art on my walls and I try to make what I can to personalise the cottage.' As she said that, she ran her hand over the quilts and her cardigan too.

She showed me around her kitchen. It was big, but I guess she needed a gigantic kitchen, and she had pots bubbling away. 'Oh, no! The time,' she said. 'I need to get on with dinner. Best you go pick fruit for the neighbours and I will see you soon for tea, ok, love?'

'Sure, thanks for the tour,' I said as I took the bags from her. I spent ages collecting fruit. It was so relaxing. I debated with myself whether I should show Paul my little Barbara collection. I needed to wait a little bit longer. I walked next door, but there was no one at home, so I wrote them a note, attached it to the fruit, and put it on their doorstep. I was getting a lot of use out of my little handbag, even if it was just to leave notes and take photos.

# Chapter Nine
## The Truth

Everything was quite normal until after dinner, when Barbara had gone home.

Paul called me on the walkie talkies when I was doing more reading in bed.

'Little sis, come in. Little sis, over.'

'Hi Paul, over.'

'Do you like Barbara? Do you think she will make me happy in twenty years? Is she the one for me? What does love mean, anyway? Do we have anything in common? Over.'

Paul was babbling, asking me all these questions straight after each other, and I had no time to answer him, even if I knew how to answer.

'Kaylee, are you there?'

I had become silent. 'Kaylee?'

'Any chance you can come to my room? Over.' Whoa, Paul's anxious.

I got out of bed and booted up the computer, then took down the *good night* sign I had up for Mason before Paul arrived, his normally perfect hair all messy.

'Are you asking because you have cold feet or are you worried about something?' I asked carefully.

Paul's shoulders dropped. 'With Barbara, it just kind of happened. There were never any sparks. I never asked her to date me or marry me, for that matter. She took control and told me it was how it was. I never thought of it until I met Erin. My heart skips a beat just thinking about her. We can talk for hours about nothing, and she is so natural. We want the same things in life, to travel and see places no one has written about. The more I try to slow down the wedding, the more aggressive Barbara gets, too. I saw a glimpse of a scary Barbara this last week.'

'Me too.' I winced, then pointed to the edge of my bed. 'Please sit, Paul. You will be shocked and hurt by what I am about to show you, sorry,' I whispered, and then played the recording of Barbara yelling at the van.

Paul froze, his only movement was his blinking eyes. After some time, he regained the ability to move and speak and he asked more about it, so I showed him the rest of my Barbara file.

Finally, I showed Paul the photo of her kissing her flatmate.

'Oh my gosh, I have been well and truly played, haven't I?' he fumed. 'The man she is kissing was meant to be gay, so I never questioned their closeness. No wonder we were having no physical relationship till after we wed, because she was already having one. Crap, I even paid for them to go on holiday together and bought the furniture in their flat and oh, so much more. I was single-handedly paying for their life together,' he said.

'Not single-handedly. Sorry, Paul,' I added, 'I think Dad has been paying too. The other day, she was coming out of Dad's office. I have also seen her asking Dad for money on your behalf and that was before you announced your engagement. Since then, Dad has given her lots of money for the engagement party.'

'Wait here,' Paul said, stomping out, slamming my door as he left.

Twenty minutes later, Paul came back with both his and Dad's cheque books. He was on the phone to the bank cancelling any written cheques.

As he hung the phone up, he said, 'Well I just saved 20,000, shame about all the rest we have lost though, but mark my words, Kaylee, she will not do this to anyone ever again.'

Paul set his computer next to mine, and he copied all my files onto his laptop. We spent the next few hours going through, searching for the name of the unpaid bills and anything else we could find on the internet. Eventually, we discovered her name was not Barbara at all, from what we could tell she had several alias names. Barbara, Belinda, or whoever she was, was a con artist (obviously). She had been doing minor crimes for years and everything (and I mean everything) she had ever told Paul was a lie. The peculiar thing was, Paul seemed relieved and not upset at all. He just had to work out how to solve the situation.

I, on the other hand, was upset. How could she treat him like this? I was mad.

Paul said not to mention it to anyone yet and that he would deal with it. 'Our secret. Now off to bed, sweetheart.' He kissed me on the head and turned my light off.

As soon as he was gone, I jumped up and turned the light on again, stepping over to the window.

*What's wrong?* Mason wrote.

*So much,* I replied.

*Can I help?*

*I wish, distract me,* I wrote.

We then spent the next twenty minutes making shadow puppets. Thanks to Mason, I went to bed smiling.

The following day was a normal day. During breakfast, Barbara called several times and Paul answered as he normally would. I overheard Paul talking to Dad about Barbara. 'Dad, if Barbara asks for any money, please only write a cheque for her. I will cancel it later. She is not who we thought she was, but I have to fly. For now, act normally towards her, please.' Then he dashed out the door. Dad turned to me.

'What on earth was that all about?' he muttered.

'He will tell you when he has his head around it all,' I said.

Dad seemed surprised. 'Oh,' he managed. 'Well, back to the office. Love you. Will you be okay at home alone today?' He asked.

'Sure, I have the neighbours and Pepe to hang out with. And if they're busy, I have a terrific book,' I said.

'Great. See you tonight, love.' With that, he too was gone.

As it was the beginning of the school holidays, there would be a lot of days like this where Dad and Paul would go off to work. So, I would chill out.

This morning, I planned on finding a quiet spot in the fruit garden and reading. It would be two months before I would start school or ballet classes, so making new friends would have to wait. Although with all the changes that have been happening, I think having some time out to *find myself* could be a wonderful thing.

I slipped upstairs to collect my book, and by the time I came down, Amber was at our door.

'Thanks for all the fruit,' she continued by saying. 'Hey, you want to hang out today?'

'Sure, that would be great. Do you have anything in mind?' I replied.

First, I showed her the gardens Pepe had shown me yesterday. She loved it there too. he ran home to get her book, and together we lay under the trees and read for over an hour. Every so often, Pepe would pop out to hang some washing out or pick some fruit. I told Amber about Barbara or whatever her name was. As I was telling Amber about all the alias names, and the money she had scammed out of Dad and Paul, we heard a shuffling noise.

'I knew it,' came a voice from behind some trees. Oops, I was not meant to have told anyone, but it was nice talking to Pepe and Amber about it. As it turned out, Pepe had suspected Barbara for a while, and she too had a file on her. We headed into the house and scanned and emailed Pepe's information to Paul, too. Paul forgave me for my big mouth. 'I am getting her back as we speak,' he said on the phone. 'I have the debt collector around emptying their flat, selling all the goods which I paid for and having the locks changed as the lease is under my name. So far, I have recovered another $20,000.'

He sounded so smug with himself. I loved it. We hung up, and I spent the rest of the day with Amber. We read some more, swam, and stretched our legs on a long walk around the neighbourhood where Amber pointed out all the important spots to me, including where we would have ballet classes together next year. I was surprised at how much I did not want to be alone. As much as I'd tried to convince myself, I felt glad to have met Amber.

On our way home from our walk, Amber waved at some girls from school; they joined us, chatty girls, and the four of us went out for ice cream. It seemed much easier for me to fit in here than I'd thought it would be. I even exchanged cell phone numbers with the girls, as they had invited me to go to the movies with them later on in the week. When we got back to my place, Amber taught me some of the dance moves she had been learning lately at dance class and thankfully, I picked them up quickly.

# Chapter Ten
## End of the Rainbow

That evening, all the fun and games started at 4.30 p.m.

Barbara was the first home after work. She told us she had come straight to our place, not surprising as she would not have gotten in at her flat.

She was sitting at the table with quotes for wedding dresses, invitations, venues, and a few other wedding items.

Betcha she was hoping to get lots of cheques from Dad.

Cow!

When Paul got home, he had a file with him (I knew it was all his information about Barbara, or whoever she was. I assumed Paul knew her real name by now), including her other identities and the relationship she had with her so-called gay flatmate.

Paul asked Barbara to go take a walk in the garden with him. She was confused but followed, anyway.

I called out, 'See you at tea.'

Barbara said, 'Sure, see you then,' but they did not return by dinner time.

Pepe and I kept exchanging concerned stares.

By the time eight-thirty came, I was really worried. I had helped Pepe wash the dishes, which had killed a bit of time.

Not wanting to head upstairs again, I settled in the lounge fiddling my fingers. Now and then, Dad would look up from the news and ask, 'Are you ok, Kaylee?' or, 'What is with you tonight?'

It was nine o'clock when Barbara came in the door alone. I was deeply shocked. I had not expected to see her again; I tried to hide my surprise. Before she spoke, I pressed the record button on my phone. She looked different, so Paul must have spoken to her.

Barbara said, 'Paul and I are back, and he said all the wedding planning has given him a headache, so he has gone to bed early. However, we have chosen the invitations, and he asked me to get a cheque for $2000 to cover the deposit and $8000 for mine and Kaylee's dress deposit. Paul said he would sort the money out with you later. I um, I feel awkward asking you this.'

I felt like coughing bull shit but held it together.

Pepe looked over, and I signalled for her to let it ride.

Dad stuck with Paul's plan and disappeared to get his cheque book. Pepe and I chatted about plum jam in the kitchen to kill the silence.

Dad wrote the cheque but of course, Barbara could not remember the name of the printers so asked him to leave it blank, which he trustingly did.

Paul didn't have a headache at all, so I ran to his room. It was, as I suspected, empty, so I called him, and his phone went straight to voice message.

I texted him on my cell phone and my watch. Nothing. No reply. I was really worried, so I grabbed my laptop and ran next door.

I explained everything to Amber, Erin, and the boys. Erin sent Jack and Mason out to take photos of Barbara's (or whatever her name was) apartment or, as they had found out the previous night, it was rented under Paul's name. I had found the new key in his room.

Erin sent me home, and I was told to text if I heard anything, and the boys would text if they found his trail.

Which they did. The non-gay flatmate was trying to climb through a window. The boys called the police, and the flatmate had to run off.

Thirty minutes later, he came back to collect his car.

Barbara and Paul were nowhere to be seen. When the flatmate had driven away, the boys climbed upstairs. The apartment was empty, only rubbish and clothes left behind. They had a hunt for any clues and found some old bills under an alias name, so they collected that, and some other things they thought may come in handy.

I could not sleep, so I spent half the night searching the alias names including the new ones. Barbara's names all started with B, Belle, Beth, and Brittany, the men were all C's Chris, Cane and Carl, and the last names always started with H, Hooper,

Harrison, and Hunt. I finally fell asleep around midnight on my couch.

At 3.15 a.m., I woke to feel my wrist vibrating. It was a message from Paul.

*Barbara and her husband have kidnapped me.*

'Where are you?' I replied. My blood ran cold, but this was not the time to lose my head.

*Don't know. I was hit on the head and have only just come around. I can smell wet damp air, and I am lying in moss,* he wrote back.

*You must be in Auckland as I am in range to write on the watch with you.*

*I think I may be in Titirangi, as I can see ferns like the ones in the Waitakere ranges, and you saw them out here the other day.*

*Their real names are Belle Harrick and Chris Haywood. They are married. Can you search for any properties under their alias in the Waitakere ranges?* Paul wrote again,

*They have written a ransom note and will deliver it with the morning's paper;*

they have taken my photo with today's paper.

I will take the note out of the letterbox. It will throw Barbara off.

Good thinking, sister.

They have moved everything out of the apartment. Jack and Mason got photos of it for us. Went through their rubbish and found more alias names.

I texted Erin, telling her what had happened. She said she would get up and come over and help. I said no, but please be ready to go look for Paul when I find some addresses, so Erin got up and dressed and the boys did too, then they catnapped in the lounge until they heard from me around 5 a.m.

I had found a house out in Laingholm just past Titirangi, which belonged to Belle and Chris Haywood, so I called Erin.

'Erin, I found it,' I told her, giving her all the details.

'Kaylee, how are you holding up over there? Do you want one of us to come and sit with you?' Mason asked.

'Thanks, Mason, but please go save my brother.'

'Will do,' he said.

'Thanks.'

I wanted to go save Paul, but if I could not go, I was glad Erin and her brothers were going.

I climbed what was becoming my favourite fruit tree, the fig tree, and waited for the newspaper to be dropped off. I had to rub my eyes, as I thought I was seeing things, but it was Barbara. Snapping away with my camera, I was getting lots more evidence on her.

As I was climbing down the tree, Pepe came out of her cottage armed with a baseball bat. 'What in plums sauce are you doing up a tree at this hour of the morning, young lady?'

'Barbara has kidnapped Paul, and she delivered a ransom note. I took photos. I am going to get rid of the note to confuse her,' I replied.

I was a bit taken back when Pepe's reaction was to give me an enormous hug and say, 'That's my girl.'

Pepe made me sit in her kitchen while she made me herbal tea and I told her everything. It must've been half an hour 'til I was able to get out of there and back on track with my mission.

I loaded the photo of Barbara walking past the house, putting an envelope in the mailbox, off to Paul's email.Wearing gloves, I carefully opened the note without touching it so as not to damage any fingerprints.

The note which had been in the envelope included a current photo of Paul with the day's newspapers. It said...

Dear Mr Edwards
If you want to see your son again, please do the following:
Take out $1,000,000.
Take it back to your house and await further instructions.
We are watching you.
DO NOT involve the police.

Paul's room was my first stop. I sent Dad an email from Paul saying he had gone to work and would see him later, which was what Paul had asked me to do.

Paul also asked me to email a police officer friend of his with all the information in the file on his computer. It had doubled since I'd last seen it.

Lots of other scans about the scams.

From what I heard later, while I was doing all that, Erin, Jack, and Mason were arriving at the address in Laingholm that I'd given them. Erin parked up the road a bit, which she needed to anyway. The roads were so narrow and windy, and they proceeded to the house.

They told me it was an old cottage that looked tiny, like only one or two bedrooms. Erin texted me: *We're here, can only see a house so far, we are heading around the back looking for a shed.*

*Paul had told me he was in a crumbly shed. It was very dark and damp.* I text back and he kept giving me instructions and just chatting as distraction; I wanted to tell Dad but he was insistent.

Later, they told me the three of them looked for a good ten minutes and could find nothing. Then Mason found a door under the cottage which had a padlock on it. Paul had already told me it was padlocked, so they had taken our bolt cutters and a crowbar with them.

Chris came out of the cottage with some food for Paul.

As Chris unlocked the door, Jack and Mason jumped on him from each side. Erin went and got Paul out and the boys replaced Chris in Paul's spot. Locking Chris up, they told him to sit tight, as the police would arrive soon.

Paul had called the police and told them everything as they drove home, and he messaged me they would arrive just after nine.

Back in Orakei, when Dad strolled out to get his paper, naturally there was no envelope in the letterbox. He carried on his morning as normal.

Barbara arrived at the same time she would usually, 7.30 a.m. She paused when she saw Dad was fine, and calmly reading the paper. I took a few secret photos, on my spy camera, of her, before joining the conversation.

'Hi, Barbara. Lovely day, isn't it? What's the daily news, Dad?' I said in a chirpy voice.

Barbara looked like a truck had hit her. 'Is Paul upstairs?' she asked in a wary voice.

'Did he forget to tell you, too? He had an important business meeting today and headed in early to set up. He sent me an email,' Dad replied.

'Oh,' she said, 'Well, I have plans to follow up. I'd better be on my way, too. See you tonight then.'

'Bye. Enjoy this glorious weather,' I called after her.

But Barbara got as far as the bottom of the stairs before Paul, Erin, and the police were standing at the door. 'Arrest her,' Paul said. 'I believe my wonderful sister here has emailed you all the evidence.'

'What in Pete's sake is going on here, Paul?' our dad asked.

'Oh, not much, just Belle, not Barbara, here and her husband Chris were conning us. They even kidnapped me last night, but thanks to your wonderful sleuthing daughter, fabulous neighbours and these nifty spy watches, Belle and her hubby will not be getting away with any more fraud,' he replied with a cheesy grin on his face.

The police took Belle away. Weird, but she never said another word. No protests. No, *it wasn't me* or *sorry* or anything. She had a poker face and was silent.

Paul, Erin, Amber, Jack, Mason, and I all followed Dad into the rumpus room, where we found comfy seats and recapped our stories from the night.

Dad was like a broken record, repeating words like, How? Under my house? Do I know anything? And he made me promise to tell him no matter how attention-seeking something may sound, he wanted to know what was going on in my life from now on.

Paul and Erin drove to the cottage in Titirangi and got the belongings Paul had paid for over the years and put them all on online sales. They made enough money that Paul bought the neighbours all a spy watch each, and now we were all connected.

Paul and Dad had taken the day off and the two families ventured to Rainbow's End for the day. We entered the adventure park and paired off as seemed our new way — Erin and Paul, Jack and Mason, Amber and me and the parents. We all did the bumper boats together, the older four did the rollercoaster and the Sky Drop, then we finished with a relaxing but competitive game of mini golf, which the Edwards won.

As the park closed, we headed back to the car, laughing and chatting as we walked.

Paul was holding Erin's hand, and they were looking at each other all gooey. The fireworks between them showed they had a connection.

Mason was beside me now. He was checking on me to make sure I was okay. I thought that was a really sweet thing.

I couldn't have picked better neighbours. Every one of these guys had gone above and beyond for us, and we hadn't known them long.

I hugged Mason to thank him for what he did, but also for being so sweet and caring.

Before we reached the cars, Paul pulled me aside and gave me a clock charm. 'Thanks for saving me, sis.'

I put one arm around Dad and the other around my big brother and said, 'I think I am going to enjoy living in Auckland.'

# Acknowledgements

Tonchi, Marco, Lucas, and Frankie you are my everything.

Special thanks to Val, Diana and Glen, thanks for your constant support.

Anna McKersey - I wouldn't have shared any of my writing without your encouragement.

Melody Lindsey, Vicki Arnott and Melissa Guyon for your fabulous editing and teaching me along the way.

Ashley Lindsay for helping me finesse and enrich my ideas.

The members of the Scriptorium, Ashley, Nicolas, Jessica, Jade, Shan, Claire, Sarah, Mayur and Kynan for all your wisdom, friendship, and inspiration.

Cassie Hart – thanks for being my constant cheerleader.

To International Writers Workshop, Writers Cafe, the Auckland Writers, RWNZ (Romance Writers of New Zealand), NZSA (New Zealand Society of Authors) and Storyline for all you have taught me at conferences and workshops and the friends and support I have met along the way.

To all the Arts of Development Performers. Thanks for your stories and helping me keep my pulse on the thoughts of today's youth.

To my beta readers Lucas, Katie, Marco, Frankie and Jazmine

Thanks to my cover artist Anas Jidar.

# Other Publications
## By Sue Carpenter

The Black Manor

Belinda's uncle has taught her everything she knows about animals but when he suddenly dies, has he taught her enough to be able to run his pet business? Belinda suspects her uncle's staff are up to more than just breeding parrots so now she has to learn to care for new animals. Caged kiwis and strange sounding boxes have Belinda on edge. What secrets are the staff hiding; are her family and animals safe?

The Summer Job

Sandra is determined to prove herself as she tries out for a summer lifesaving job – a job that will take her away from the safety of the farm into the unknown. But Sandra isn't expecting to meet someone who will change her life. She soon discovers that people can be manipulative and deceitful. Will she navigate the turbulent waters of first love and a new job.

Lavender and Pearls

Jackie and her brother Hayden are sent to stay at their eccentric aunt's antique shop in New Zealand, where they discover a magical secret. When her family members start to go missing, Jackie must venture into fantastical and dangerous new lands to save them. Will Jackie rescue her family? And what secrets will she discover along the way?

The Dramatic Bubble

Kenzie wants to focus on her school exams with no distractions, but cupid, COVID and the government have other ideas. Will the Catholic boy be a distraction for her, or the only thing that holds her together as her family life collapses?

# Sue Carpenter

Sue is a Junior Fiction and Young Adult Author.

She had learning issues growing up, but an active imagination. As an adult she doesn't want her readers to need a dictionary to fall into her imaginary worlds.

Sue is not ready to grow up yet and keeps her mind young by writing for children and spending time with her three sons.

To find more of Sue's work follow her on Instagram and Tik Tok susieleenz